It's Christmas Eve, and Father Christmas should be coming – but

Fairy book should

Can Ellie and Max save Christmas for the world?

Let battle begin!

Jeremy Strong once worked in a bakery, putting the jam into three thousand doughnuts every night. Now he puts the jam in stories instead, which he finds much more exciting. At the age of three, he fell out of a first-floor bedroom window and landed on his head. His mother says that this damaged him for the rest of his life and refuses to take any responsibility. He loves writing stories because he says it is 'the only time you alone have complete control and can make anything happen'. His ambition is to make you laugh (or at least snuffle). Jeremy Strong lives near Bath with his wife, Gillie, four cats and a flying cow.

Are you feeling silly enough to read more?

THE HUNDRED-MILE-AN-HOUR DOG
RETURN OF THE HUNDRED-MILE-AN-HOUR DOG
WANTED! THE HUNDRED-MILE-AN-HOUR DOG
LOST! THE HUNDRED-MILE-AN-HOUR DOG

MY DAD'S GOT AN ALLIGATOR!
MY GRANNY'S GREAT ESCAPE
MY MUM'S GOING TO EXPLODE!
MY BROTHER'S FAMOUS BOTTOM
MY BROTHER'S FAMOUS BOTTOM GETS PINCHED!
MY BROTHER'S FAMOUS BOTTOM GOES CAMPING

INVASION OF THE CHRISTMAS PUDDINGS

LAUGH YOUR Socks off with

Jeremy STRONG

The Battle for Christmas

Illustrated by Rowan Clifford

PUFFIN

Published by the Penguin Group
Penguin Books Ltd, 80 Strand, London WC2R 0RL, England
Penguin Group (USA) Inc., 375 Hudson Street, New York, New York 10014, USA
Penguin Group (Canada), 90 Eglinton Avenue East, Suite 700, Toronto, Ontario, Canada M4P 2Y3
(a division of Pearson Penguin Canada Inc.)
Penguin Ireland, 25 St Stephen's Green, Dublin 2, Ireland (a division of Penguin Books Ltd)
Penguin Group (Australia), 250 Camberwell Road, Camberwell, Victoria 3124, Australia
(a division of Pearson Australia Group Pty Ltd)
Penguin Books India Pvt Ltd, 11 Community Centre, Panchsheel Park, New Delhi – 110 017, India
Penguin Group (NZ), 67 Apollo Drive, Rosedale, North Shore 0632, New Zealand
(a division of Pearson New Zealand Ltd)
Penguin Books (South Africa) (Pty) Ltd, 24 Sturdee Avenue, Rosebank, Johannesburg 2196, South Africa

Penguin Books Ltd, Registered Offices: 80 Strand, London WC2R 0RL, England

puffinbooks.com

First published 2008
1

Text copyright © Jeremy Strong, 2008
Illustrations copyright © Rowan Clifford, 2008
All rights reserved

The moral right of the author and illustrator has been asserted

Set in MT Baskerville
Made and printed in England by Clays Ltd, St Ives plc

British Library Cataloguing in Publication Data
A CIP catalogue record for this book is available from the British Library

ISBN: 978-0-141-32463-0

www.greenpenguin.co.uk

This is for Mr Beynon,
my long-suffering first bank manager.
I hope that wherever you are I may have put
a smile on your face at last.

Contents

1 So Joseph put Mary on a Dinosaur . . .

This is Ellie, aged ten. She's pulling a face because Dad told her to smile. Ellie thinks she doesn't look like she feels, which is cool, sophisticated, beautiful and clever. Instead she reckons she has far too many freckles, is too short, has big feet and looks childish.

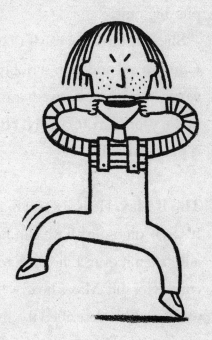

Ellie was born the day before Christmas, and her parents nearly

1

decided that they would call her 'Christmas'. Ellie is very glad they didn't call her that because she says that if they had she might have had to kill them.

'Ellie!' gasped Mum, horrified.

'It's a joke, Mum,' Ellie explained patiently.

You might think that having your birthday so close to Christmas would make everything twice as much fun. It doesn't, and Ellie thinks it's the pits, big time.

She gets birthday cards that have and *happy Christmas too*! added in scribbly felt tip. Even worse, most people give her one present, saying that it's for Christmas AND birthday. How mean is that? Ask Ellie.

This is Max. He is six and mad about dinosaurs. It's as if dinosaurs have climbed into his brain and taken it over. Ellie once told Mum that if you cut the top off Max's head – 'like a boiled egg' was how Ellie described it – and looked inside

you'd see hundreds of tiny dinosaurs running round and round. They'd be chasing one another, leaping and clawing, fighting and biting like mad things. Hundreds of them.

Mum said it was an utterly blood-curdling idea

and Ellie shouldn't be so horrible. Ellie groaned.

'It's a joke, Mum. I said IF you cut off the top of his head. I didn't say DO IT. I said IF, and that means no blood.'

Ellie reckons her parents have no idea at all. 'I do love Max,' she told Dad. 'But I like to show it by trying to kill him. He's such a noodle.'

Having a birthday on Christmas Eve was inconvenient, but Ellie was still managing to have a good time. Mum and Dad were in the kitchen, surrounded by dirty pots and pans, not to mention piles of food, as they geared up for the Christmas Day feast. Ellie reckons her dad is the best cook in the world and Mum is second. Max says Mum is best and Dad is second. This gives both children a good excuse to try and kill each other again which, as you know, they enjoy.

'I can do karate,' said Max, waving his arms about threateningly. Ellie shrugged.

'I only do Instant Death,' she warned, leaving

Max wishing that he was ten and Ellie was six.

Mum tried to keep things nice and peaceful by telling Max the Christmas story. She had just got to the bit where wicked King Herod appears on the scene.

'He sent his soldiers to find the baby,' said Mum. 'Mary and Joseph had to run away, so Mary climbed on to a –'

'Dinosaur!' Max burst out, sending Dad into fits of chuckles.

'And you can stop laughing,' Mum warned him. 'No, a donkey. They left the country and went into Egypt. Meanwhile, the Three Wise –'

'Dinosaurs?' Ellie suggested brightly, before Max could, so he launched an attack.

Mum threw them an irritated glance. 'I don't think you two are very interested in this story,' she muttered.

'That's because we've heard it a trillion times and Max isn't bothered because it hasn't got any tyrannosaurs in it.'

Ellie was pretty much right about this. Both she and Max secretly thought the Christmas story would be a lot more interesting if it had dinosaurs in it, or whales. She was the one who liked whales, especially the ones that sing – humpback whales. The stable should have had dinosaurs and whales in it. Ellie said that King Herod's soldiers would never have gone snooping around if they thought they might be attacked by humpback whales and some dinosaurs.

Fortunately there was a ring at the door at that point. It turned out to be the postman with a parcel for Ellie, wrapped in brown paper and string. The stamps looked rather exotic and used an alphabet that nobody in the family recognized. The crackly paper gave off a faint smell of rainforest and sandalwood. Or maybe it was the pong of damp gorilla fur and woodsmoke. It was magical and mysterious and made Ellie's heart beat faster.

Inside the parcel Ellie found a jacket and a pair of trousers. They were made of cotton and covered with a pattern of little pictures – pirates, princesses, unicorns, dinosaurs, buildings, palm tree islands and more all jostled for space.

'I think they're pyjamas,' Dad murmured. 'Who sent them, anyway?'

Ellie rescued a badly scribbled note from the crumpled packaging.

WARNING! These are COSMIC PYJAMAS. I found them at the back of a tiny shop, down a tiny alley, off a tiny square, on a tiny street, in a tiny Turkish town.

Legend says you must never wear the top and bottom at the same time. I didn't have time to find out why not.

I don't know why they're Cosmic either. I just liked the pictures.

HAPPY BIRTHDAY! HAPPY CHRISTMAS!

Fond love from Great-Aunt Jemima.

'Oh well,' sighed Mum. 'That explains everything. Great-Aunt Jemima's as daft as a brush.'

Dad disagreed. 'She just likes exploring and adventure. I think she's a rather splendid old lady.'

Ellie wasn't listening. She stood holding the strange nightwear, turning them over in her hands and staring at them. What on earth were Cosmic Pyjamas?

2 Max and Ellie Go Christmas Shopping

If someone gives you a pair of pyjamas and makes a point of telling you not to wear the top at the same time as the bottoms, what is the first thing you want to do? Exactly. You want to wear both bits. Besides, Ellie reckoned she'd look pretty daft wearing just the bottom half, and she'd look even more daft if she only wore the top. Anyhow, she wanted to see what they looked like and she could only do that by trying on both parts at the same time.

BAD MISTAKE! (But she didn't realize that, yet.)

Ellie looked in her mirror. She didn't think she would win any fashion prizes but she did have to admit that the pyjamas made her feel strange.

She put this down to all the crazy stuff Great-Aunt Jemima had written in her note. Her head was feeling all jumbled, as if everything inside was being stirred up and shaken.

Ellie sat on the edge of her bed and fiddled with her recorder, *squeak squeak*. She hadn't been learning the recorder for long, and it showed. Even her recorder teacher, Mrs Tompkinson, sent her outside to practise. Mrs Tompkinson once told Ellie that when Ellie played the recorder it sounded as if she was treading on several cats and the odd piglet or two. Strange to say, Ellie didn't find that very encouraging.

As she idly squeaked and squawked she glanced at the little pictures on her sleeve. There was a dinosaur, galloping along, and beside it a winged horse. She found the planet Saturn – the one with rings round it. Next to that was a small shop with a sign above the window that said: CHRISTMAS SHOP. Ellie was just looking at that when the tiny door of the shop opened.

THE DOOR OF THE SHOP ON THE PYJAMAS OPENED!

Ellie blinked like mad, looked again and it shut, opened and then shut once more. She slowly got to her feet, holding her left arm as far away from her body as possible, as if it was covered in some terrible infection. She moved slowly out to the landing and across to Max's room.

'Max?' she whispered, her voice sounding odd and croaky. 'The door just opened.'

'Shut it behind you on your way out,' Max said pointedly.

'Max, you don't understand. The door opened. The door of the shop.'

'Go away.'

'Max! The door! Of the shop! It opened!'

Max at last looked up from the dinosaur book he was studying.

'Did you know that the really big dinosaurs had two brains? One to move their tails and one —'

'Max, look at the shop!' howled Ellie.

'Don't get your knickers in a twist,' Max said evenly, getting off his bed. 'Why are you holding out your arm like that?'

'Just look at the shop on the sleeve,' pleaded Ellie. 'Tell me I'm not dreaming. Tell me I'm not mad. The door of the shop opens and shuts.'

Max stood next to her and they both stared at the little picture. The door remained firmly shut. A smile crept on to Max's face.

'You're a –' he
began, but he didn't
finish. His mouth
stayed open. The
door of the shop
remained shut
but instead all the
coloured Christmas
lights in the shop
window came on and
began flickering.
Max grabbed
Ellie's arm in
amazement, his
eyes goggling and
then –
BLAMMM!
KERRANNGGG!!
PHWOOOOOSSHHH!!!
They both disappeared
into whirling blackness. All

they could do was cling to each other, yelling and screaming, as they were hurled along in the dark. It was like being on a helter-skelter that was going down a mega-gigantic water flume, with all the lights out. And then suddenly −

FFWWAAAAHHHHHHHH!!!!

Colours spun around them. They were tumbling giddily over and over in space and then they landed on something hard and skidded along the ground until they came up against a wall that stopped them in their tracks. BANG!

'Ouch!'

For a second they lay there, dazed and winded.

Then, just as they began to struggle to sit up, an avalanche of brightly coloured giant balls rained down on them. They bounced off their heads, shoulders, arms and legs before rolling away in all directions. At last they stopped and the two children opened their eyes.

It was dark. They took in quick, deep gulps of air, and flicked their eyes round their new surroundings.

'Are we dead?' Max asked.

'Yes, Max,' Ellie answered, rubbing her bottom. 'That's why we can talk to each other.'

Max grinned. 'Cool! I'm dead!' His sister decided it was best if she ignored him. Sometimes he could be very annoying.

'Where are we?' he asked.

'I don't know, Max. As you can see, it's dark, so it's rather difficult to tell.'

There was a faint crackle and some tiny coloured lights flickered on for a microsecond before going off, coming back on and going off once more. They stayed off.

'They looked like Christmas-tree lights,' Ellie murmured.

'They never work,' Max snorted. 'Dad had to get new ones this year. He said our old ones were –'

Fortunately Max didn't finish. A pair of lights had just appeared and they were gradually inching towards the children, accompanied by a faint whirring noise. Max shifted closer to his sister.

'What is it?' he whispered.

'Just keep still and quiet. Mummy will look after you.'

Max elbowed her in the ribs. 'I don't need looking after. I can do karate,' he boasted, rather half-heartedly.

A mechanical clumping sound echoed in the still air and the lights swivelled towards them. Ellie was scared and gripped her recorder tightly. It was all she had to defend herself and Max with

– a plastic recorder. What a deadly weapon! On the other hand maybe she could scare whatever-it-was away with some squashed piglet noises. Ellie shaded her eyes from the glare and stumbled to her feet. She reckoned they might have to run for safety. Whatever it was had almost reached them.

The whirring stopped and the lights focused directly on the children. They got the distinct impression that they were both being closely examined.

'Oh. Carol singers.'

That was what the thing said, in a deep, slightly grumpy voice. The lights began to turn away from them and head back and as they did the faulty Christmas lights flickered briefly. There, caught in the multicoloured glimmer, they could see what it was that had been looking at them.

A DINOSAUR.

Or, to be more exact, it was a diplodocus, as

Max the Dinosaur Expert was quick to point out. But he was also puzzled.

'The diplodocus,' he whispered, 'did not have eyes that shone in the dark. And they are supposed to be much bigger than we are. This one is titchy.'

Ellie had a different answer. 'Suppose the dinosaur is the right size and somehow we have been made much, much bigger than we were.'

'Like giants?' asked Max. 'Cool! I'm in the Land of Dinosaurs and I'm a giant.'

Ellie rolled her eyes. 'There are a couple of other little things I'd like to point out about that dinosaur,' she said. 'It spoke. It seemed to think we are carol singers. Also, it had tinsel wrapped round its neck. Now it seems to me we have a problem there. Why would a dinosaur wear tinsel round its neck, why would it talk and why would it think we were carol singers?'

Max considered all this for a few moments. The answer was simple. 'Because it's Christmas,' he said.

'Max, it can't be a real dinosaur.'

'Oh.' There was no doubt that Ellie's little brother was disappointed. 'Uncool,' he added. 'I guess it must be some kind of toy.'

Ellie was shaking with the enormity of what had happened to them. If Max was right and the dinosaur was a toy, then they had to face a different problem all together. Nobody, but nobody made toys as big as dinosaurs. Ellie delivered her shattering conclusion.

'In that case, we're not giants,' she gulped. 'In fact, quite the opposite has happened. Max, we've been shrunk.'

3 Who's a Mince Spy?

While Max and Ellie were discussing the finer points of dinosaur recognition, a crowd of shadowy figures silently gathered around the children and began to press forward. The two children were being surrounded. Peering into the dark, broken only by the brief fizzing

of the patchy lights, Ellie tried to make out
what they were. Penguins. A triceratops and a
tyrannosaur. A pair of giraffes, three teddy bears,
a group of carol singers, half a dozen Marys, the
same number of Josephs and four donkeys. (The
other two had been kidnapped, as Max and Ellie
would later discover.)

Ellie grasped Max's arm. 'I know where we
are! What were we doing when everything
vanished and we were swept off our feet?'

'Looking at a picture on your stupid pyjamas.

Can I play with the dinosaurs?'

'No. Listen, Max. The door opened, the window lights came on and flash bang! That's where we must be now. In the Christmas Shop. Everything here is a Christmas toy or decoration. Those giant balls that fell on us – they were just like Christmas-tree baubles. We must have dislodged them from their shelf when we crashed up against the wall.'

'Cool!' grinned Max. 'We're in Christmas Land!'

By this time thirty or more toys had gathered round, together with some decorations – the things that hang on Christmas trees or get stuck in the icing on festive cakes. There were reindeer, polar bears and Father Christmases. In addition to that lot, a crowd of Christmas-stocking toys jostled with a flock of sheep from a nativity set and several pairs of wind-up clacking false teeth.

Two glitzy dolls pushed their way through the shifting crowd and confronted Ellie and

Max. They took up a threatening stance. One
was impossibly blonde, wearing a jazzy pair
of denim shorts, high heels and a T-shirt with
a silver lightning bolt design on the front. She
had a knife strapped to one thigh and a sparkly
handbag hanging from her right shoulder. She
was chewing gum and rolling it round her mouth.

'It's Lara Croft gone blonde,' Max whispered excitedly.

'With a handbag like that she's more like Lara Barbie, if you ask me,' Ellie hissed back.

The second doll had long, impossibly glossy black hair, a red bandana round her head and a matching red eyepatch over her left eye. She was dressed in a leopardskin-print catsuit and a short sarong, with a wide, loose belt studded with fake diamonds. Something bulky hung from the belt.

'Wow! She's got a gun.' Max pointed at the holster. 'Neat!'

Max was so excited by the gun that he didn't even seem to realize that the doll had one leg missing. She was using a rainbow pencil as a crutch. Ellie couldn't help noticing that the doll had left a multicoloured dotted trail behind her.

The blonde doll took a step forward, one hand resting on the handle of her knife.

'Name's Commander Blondie, Double "O" Heaven,' she announced, tossing back her thick mane and staring intently at Ellie and Max with startlingly blue eyes. 'This 'ere is Commander Aysha. Are you rebels?'

Ellie turned up both hands and shrugged. 'I don't think so. We've only just arrived here.'

Aysha lifted her eyepatch and carried out a closer inspection. 'They don't look like anyone from round here, sister,' she muttered, before replacing the eyepatch. Evidently it was a fashion item and not of any real use.

Aysha unbuttoned her holster, whipped out a tube of deep-red lipstick and trailed it round her mouth. She popped the lipstick back, checked her make-up in a little vanity mirror and snapped the holster shut. So much for the gun. Max was bitterly disappointed.

'Well, if they ain't rebels, sister, what are they?' asked Blondie.

Max nudged Ellie. 'Why do they call each other sister? They can't be sisters, can they?'

'It's just a way of showing they work together,' Ellie explained. 'I think they're secret agents or in some kind of army. I'm going to talk to them.'

Ellie took a deep breath and began to explain what had happened. Blondie widened her eyes, flashing a massive pair of false eyelashes as she did so.

'Well, ain't that a story and a half!' she exclaimed. 'I wondered why you was still in your jimmy-jams. Where's your 'andbag, love, anyway?'

'I don't have one,' Ellie said.

Aysha flicked up her eyepatch and goggled at Ellie. 'Doesn't have a handbag! Have you ever heard the like, sister? Where do you keep your make-up then?'

'I don't have any,' Ellie admitted.

'Lord 'elp us,' muttered Blondie. 'You's a fashion disaster, you is, that's what.'

At this point the diplodocus pushed his long neck forward and muttered something into Aysha's ear. The doll frowned and nodded. 'Dippy reckons they're not carol singers after all, sister. He says they might be spies.'

The two commanders examined Max and Ellie all over again.

'Yeah, could be,' murmured Blondie, with a frown. 'That explains why they look odd. They're probably mince spies.'

Max and Ellie burst out laughing. It was not a

good thing to do.

'Stop it!' cried Blondie. 'What you laughin' at?'

'We're mince spies!' giggled Max.

Instantly half the penguins, bears and Father Christmases took several worried steps back.

'There! The boy's just admitted it,' cried Blondie in alarm. 'We got a pair of mince spies 'ere, right in our midst.'

Ellie realized that while all of this was funny to her and Max it certainly wasn't funny to *them*. They were genuinely scared.

'What exactly is a mince spy?' Ellie asked gently. 'I'm sorry if we upset you, but we don't know what you're talking about. Where we come from there is no such thing as a mince spy.'

One of the penguins pressed forward and spoke slowly and pointedly. 'Mince spies were like us once, only now they've been minced.' The penguin gave Max a very hard stare. 'Anyone might be a mince spy.'

'Who minces you?' Ellie asked.

'Who do you think?' snapped Aysha. 'Don't pretend you don't know. The Christmas Fairy.'

For a split second Ellie thought this was some kind of joke, but several penguins had tumbled over backward as they fainted from the awful

horror of what had been mentioned. Half the Father Christmases had pulled their floppy hats right down over their heads to hide.

'An' when she's finished mincin',' Blondie continued, 'she makes the toy into somefing else, like a child, for example,' she added, glaring at Ellie and Max. 'And she sends it back to spy on us.'

'But why would a Christmas fairy want to spy on you?' asked Ellie, struggling to understand.

'Are you stupid, or what?' snapped Blondie. 'It's not *a* Christmas fairy, it's THE Christmas Fairy. To find out what we're doin', an' to stop it, whatever it is. An' maybe that's why you two's 'ere. Maybe you two's spyin' for the Chris–SCRAM!' she suddenly screamed. 'Angel attack! Retreat!'

The toys vanished in all directions in panic, waddling over each other, crashing past Max and Ellie until the two children found themselves alone in the middle of a dark and empty room.

They were very puzzled and their heads were ringing with questions. Why was everyone worried about spies? And as for an angel *attack*, what was that all about? Since when had angels begun attacking people? Surely they wouldn't attack Ellie and Max, anyway? They hadn't done anything.

And then something nasty stung Ellie. And Max.

Ow! Ow! Ow!

4 Angel Wings, Angel Stings and a Very Hairy Christmas Fairy

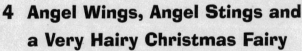

The air was filled with buzzing angels everywhere, whizzing and whirring, glittering like frost and blowing their trumpets. No – they weren't trumpets at all. They were blowpipes! The angels were swooping down in waves and zapping stings at the two children.

Max leaped up and down, waving his arms

furiously, trying to beat off the angelic host, most of whom were as big as he was. Only a few had feathery wings. The rest had to make do with crude wooden panels that slapped the air and made them the most clumsy, awkward creatures imaginable. They squeaked and shrieked to each other, zooming in like wasps descending on a picnic.

'Make them run! Make them jump! Sting, sting, sting the mince spies!'

Ellie groaned. Why did *everyone* think they were spies? She wished they'd stop calling her a mince spy too. She was beginning to feel like a bad joke that had fallen out of a Christmas cracker.

The children were slowly driven back to the wall and it wasn't long before they were pinned against it, with about fifty stinging trumpets aimed at them. In effect, they had been captured.

'What do we do now?' Max asked his big sister.

Ellie wanted to say something encouraging but she was rapidly becoming very fed up with the whole business. She snapped back at her brother. 'Funnily enough, I don't know, Max, I've never had to fight angels with nasty stings before. It's not in my *Good Girl's Guide to What to Do in Moments of Mortal Danger* either.'

'Sssilenccce!'

The new voice hissed like a snake in a frying pan. Ellie and Max found themselves gazing at what was quite obviously the angel leader. She was none other than the fairy off the Christmas tree, the one the toys were so afraid of, the one that made the penguins faint – and she didn't look happy. Her body was twisting and jerking as if she was being constantly and painfully poked.

She kept stretching one hand behind to scratch herself.

Max sniggered. 'I think she's been stuck on top of the Christmas tree too often,' he muttered. 'No wonder she keeps jerking like that. She must have such a sore bu—'

'Sssilence, ssspy!' yelled the Christmas Fairy, swiping at Max with her wand and almost taking off his left ear. 'Ssspeak when you're sssspoken to.'

Ellie knew a bully when she saw one and stepped in front of Max defensively. 'You did speak to us. You told us to be silent,' she boldly pointed out.

There's nothing like a bit of silly logic to upset bossy people. The Christmas Fairy erupted into a volcanic rage and almost blew her dress off. It took her ages to calm down and meanwhile her tatty, wooden-winged angelic army spluttered and tutted and pointed their sting-things at the children even more angrily.

Ellie kept thinking that at any moment she would wake up, but she didn't. It was no dream and there was no relief. She was just going to have to get on with it.

The Christmas Fairy eventually managed to scrape herself off the ceiling. She fixed Ellie and Max with an icy glare from one eye. The other eye was missing. In fact the more Ellie examined the Christmas Fairy, the more ancient she

seemed. Her sparkle and glitter were tarnished.
Her make-up was cracked and her lipstick
smeared into a snarling sneer. Her hair was
falling out. One shoe was missing and her dress
was torn and grubby. Ellie couldn't help thinking
that, compared to Blondie and Aysha, here was a
real fashion disaster.

'What are you doing here?' the Christmas
Fairy demanded.

'We don't know,' Ellie answered, quite
truthfully. 'We'd really rather not be here at all.
We'd like to go home because otherwise we're
going to miss Christmas. Besides, our parents
will be worried. You know what parents are like.
They get worried if you go to the toilet for longer
than half a minute. They probably think you've
drowned. In fact I sometimes –'

'Sssilenccce!' screamed the Christmas Fairy
again, and her one good eye spun round and
round in its socket. 'Where have you come from?'

Ellie whizzed through the pyjama story once

more, finishing up by telling the Christmas Fairy
that they lived in Great Britain.

A hush fell upon the angels. 'The World!'
they whispered excitedly. 'They come from The
World!'

'Shut up, you fairy cakes!' roared the Christmas
Fairy before turning back to Ellie and Max. 'Ssso
you come from The World. Do you happen to
know Father Christmas?'

The Christmas Fairy leaned forward and
peered at them very closely now, still twitching
from time to time. There was a glint in her eye
that made Ellie think the question might be a
dangerous trap. She must answer it in just the
right way or they would end up in very hot water.
Trouble was, Ellie had no idea why the question
was dangerous or what she should answer. Tricky!

'We have *heard* of Father Christmas,' she
began. 'Everyone in the world has heard of
Father Christmas, but we don't know him.'

'Hmmm.' The Christmas Fairy seemed

disappointed. Ellie felt it was a good sign. Maybe they had escaped the trap, whatever it was. Hooray!

'You've not met him then?'

'No.' Ellie shook her head.

The Fairy jerked away from them for a moment, then suddenly swung round and poked her face even closer to Ellie's. 'And what about rebels? Have you met any?'

Ellie suddenly remembered Blondie had mentioned a rebel army. But which lot *were* the rebels – the angels or Blondie and co?

'What rebels?' asked Ellie, playing it safe.

'Hrrrgh,' growled the Fairy. She was definitely puzzled now, and frustrated by Ellie's replies. She scratched her rear furiously. She ignored Ellie's question and pressed on with the interrogation. 'Ssso, if you don't know Father Christmas and you don't know any rebels, why have you come here?'

'Didn't have any choice,' Ellie shrugged. 'We

just found ourselves here.'

One of the feathered angels pressed forward. 'Blondie and The Others were trying to arrest them, Christmas Fairy.'

'Were they, indeed? They can't be spying on us then.'

'Why would we want to spy on you?' Ellie asked. 'We've only just got here and we don't know what's going on. We've been surrounded by dinosaurs and dolls and attacked by angels with stings and we still don't know why.'

'Ssspies everywhere,' muttered the Christmas Fairy. 'It's that other lot, trying to discover our —' She broke off and looked sharply at the children again. She stuck the pointed end of her wand under Ellie's chin and lifted it up. It hurt. 'Oh no, you don't. You can't trick me into giving our secrets away.'

'I really don't know what you're talking about,' Ellie choked up, as the wand pressed against her throat.

Max stuck his head out from behind his sister.
'I'm six and a half,' he complained. 'You're not
allowed to be a spy when you're only six and a
half. Everybody knows that!'

'Ssssssssh! How dare you! You teeny-weeny-
peeny thing! I could have you made into
Christmas pudding!'

Both the children shrank away from the Fairy
who, despite her anger, could not deny Max's
reasoning. Strange to say, it was one of the angels
who came to their aid.

'They're harmless,' the angel murmured to her leader. 'We're wasting our time. They don't know anything, Mistress. Might as well let them go.'

'Yessss,' hissed the Christmas Fairy. 'Let them go. They're useless to us.'

And with that they all buzzed off. In a few moments the last clattering wooden angel had vanished and the two children were by themselves once more. Ellie looked at Max.

'Have you worked out what's going on yet?' she asked.

He shook his head. 'You?'

'Nope. But maybe Commander Blondie has. Look, she's coming back, and this time she's driving a tank.'

5 Exploding Mangers and Dead Secret Plans

Blondie stood in the tank's turret, wearing a customized glitter-pink crash helmet and a frown. The tank's main cannon was swivelling around wildly in search of the recently departed enemy. It ground to a halt right in front of Ellie and Max.

'Thought you might need some 'elp,' grunted the blonde commander.

A second tank, with Aysha at the controls, sped up. The tank squeaked to a halt and the gun turret swung round so fast that it almost took Blondie's head off. She had to duck down into her own tank at lightning speed. Aysha was now sporting two designer eyepatches, one for each eye, and consequently had no idea where she was going.

'Oh!' Ellie was surprised to realize that Blondie and Aysha were on a rescue mission to save them. The last time they'd met, Ellie and Max had almost been arrested, for spying of course. Why was everyone in the shop so scared of spies?

'Them angels is nasty beasts,' the doll scowled. 'They're about as angelic as a scorpion wiv toothache.'

'I don't think scorpions can get toothache; they don't have teeth,' said Ellie and immediately felt ashamed of herself. After all, Blondie was trying to help.

'Don't matter,' shrugged the doll. 'I wouldn't like to meet a scorpion wiv or wivout teeth, so there. You two 'ad better get up 'ere in case them pesky flyin' fings come back.'

Ellie and Max climbed on to the tank and Blondie swung the vehicle round. They trundled across the floor of the empty room. Max was impressed.

'I wish I could drive it,' he sighed.

'Get your own bloomin' tank,' snapped Blondie. Ellie smiled to herself. She was beginning to like the cantankerous commander.

Before long they came to the far edge of the room. As they approached the skirting board a large panel slid to one side with a faint swoosh and the tank plunged straight through the entrance and vanished into the next room.

'Cool!' murmured Max, as they rumbled through a short tunnel before emerging into another world. Behind them a group of plastic

penguins hurriedly pushed the door back into place to conceal the entrance.

As they gazed around Ellie and Max saw all sorts of work going on. Another tank was being prepared by more penguins. A group of teddy bears was making repairs to a large fire engine. A loud bang followed by an expanding puff of drifting smoke drew their attention to a wooden nativity group. Mary, Joseph and the Three Kings had just deliberately blown up something that looked suspiciously like the Baby Jesus's manger.

Ellie swallowed hard. 'Was that an exploding crib I just saw?' she asked faintly and Blondie nodded.

'Need everyfing we can fink of,' the doll muttered darkly. 'There's a war goin' on out there an' the rebels are winnin'. Can 'ardly move anywhere wivout bein' attacked. It's like they know what we're gonna do. Like someone's tellin' 'em our secrets.' The commander gave Ellie another searching glance.

'A war? Wow! Cool!' said Max.

'Is he always like this?' growled Blondie, and Ellie apologized.

'He's only six,' she explained.

'War's not cool, child,' bustled Aysha. 'It's tough. How do you think I lost my leg?'

'I'm sorry,' murmured Ellie and fell into silence, but Max wanted to know the grim details.

'It was blown off by the Dove,' growled Blondie.

'What dove?' Max was curious. He'd never

50

thought doves were dangerous.

'Supposed to be a Dove of Peace,' snorted
Blondie. 'Hah! Christmas Fairy uses it as a
bomber. She's an evil bit of fruitcake, that one.
Aysha was on a mission wiv a couple of penguins
an' the Dove comes down an' SPLAT! Wipe out
– completely splattered. The penguins snuffed it
and she lost a leg. Nuffin' we could do.'

'Urgh!' went Max.

'It was nasty,' nodded Aysha.

'But what are you all fighting *about*?' asked
Ellie, only mildly surprised that she was talking to
a plastic doll. She seemed to have grown used to
the fact that she'd been shrunk down to the size
of a small banana and whisked away to a place
she had never dreamed of.

'Escape,' said Blondie. 'We're fightin' for our
freedom, to save Father Christmas and, to put it
bluntly, to save bloomin' Christmas for the 'ole of
your bloomin' world.'

'Wow, coo–' began Max, as Ellie clamped a

51

hand over his mouth.

They had left the tanks and were walking across to the small cluster of buildings that Blondie said were their headquarters. Inside there was a lot of talk going on. It stopped as soon as they entered. Everyone turned to stare at the two newcomers. Ellie and Max were once again the centre of attention and found themselves being carefully examined by a curious group of dinosaurs, Marys and Josephs, Father Christmases and all sorts of toys – everyone in fact that hadn't already met the two children.

'It's OK,' explained Blondie. 'They're with Aysha an' me. Christmas Fairy almost got 'em but they talked their way out of it.' Blondie nodded towards Ellie. 'She's the clever one. The other's just a baby.'

'No, I'm not!' yelled Max, outraged.

'See what I mean?' grunted the doll. She turned to Ellie. 'This is our Operations Room. Got a big battle goin' on. Fings 'ave been buildin' up to this for weeks. It's almost Christmas Day.'

'Tomorrow!' cheered Max.

'Exactly,' Aysha continued. 'Tonight Father Christmas does his rounds. He gets his toys and gifts from this shop and loads his sleigh. For us, it's our Great Day – the day we escape and are set free into your world. We become the toys of children around the globe. But this year is different. There's been trouble – a rebellion.'

'The angels?' asked Ellie, glad that one mystery had been cleared up.

'Said she was clever,' nodded Blondie, with the briefest of smiles. 'The angels don't want to be released. They 'ate Christmas. Loathe it wiv a passion.'

'Why?' asked Max. 'Nobody hates Christmas.'

'Think about it, child,' Aysha went on. 'What happens to the angels every Christmas? They get stuck on Christmas trees for twelve days and then get put in a dark box to wait for another year. It's not much fun but that's their job. At least it is supposed to be their job. Then this year that hag-bag, the Christmas Fairy, decides to put all these smart ideas in their silly heads. She's a misery she is and about as cheerful as a Christmas turkey.'

The whole room collapsed into laughter. Aysha eyed them with surprise.

'What did I say? Why is that funny?' Everyone only laughed louder and Blondie had to wait a couple of minutes before she could take up the story.

'I feel sorry for 'er really, gettin' stuck on top of the tree in the shop every year, and in that get-up too. It ain't just yesterday, it's last century. And 'er make-up! She should do somefing about that eye. Anyways, she's put this idea into the angels' 'eads that they can stop Father Christmas from collectin' us. In fact they want to stop 'im from goin' on 'is rounds at all.'

'How will they do that?' asked Ellie. 'The angels are titchy compared to Father Christmas.' A silence fell on the room.

Blondie, grim-faced, looked round at everyone there. 'We don't know,' she said at last. 'Word is that the angels are workin' on a Dead Secret Plan but that's the only info we 'ave. Aysha tried to find out an' look what 'appened to 'er. Sent in a couple more spies a few days back, a mouse an' a caterpillar on wheels. Mouse came back wiv 'alf

'er fur missin'. They'd been caught. Caterpillar put up an immense fight but lost most of 'is wheels and ended up on the mincin' pile. In the confusion Mouse escaped. They were best friends too.'

'Oh,' murmured Ellie. 'That is sad.'

'Yeah,' grunted Blondie. 'Mouse 'as these awful bald patches now. Wouldn't put my 'ead out the door wiv patches like that. I've tried to cheer 'er up – gave 'er some of my lipstick. It's not all that new – *Merry Cherry* it's called an' I don't use it no more, but Mouse wouldn't know. She's not very – you know?'

'Into fashion?' suggested Ellie.

'Exactly, like, she didn't even notice the new high heels I got last week. Anyhow, fing is, if we don't know what the Dead Secret Plan is, 'ow can we stop 'em? An' if we don't stop 'em we shan't escape an' Father Christmas will 'ave no presents to deliver an' then it's curtains for Christmas.'

Max gave his big sister a bewildered glance. 'Why would anyone want curtains for Christmas?' he asked.

Ellie let out a long sigh.

6 Mince Spies

'We must do something,' declared Max. His face
wore a large, angry frown and his little fists were

58

clenched, ready for action.

'What you gonna do?' asked Blondie, with enough of a sneer to push Ellie into reminding her that Max was only six.

'And a half,' Max added quickly. 'We could take them by surprise. Why don't we attack them in the middle of the night when they're asleep and leap on their beds and capture them all and tie them up so they can't do anything?'

''Ave you any idea what guards are for?' Blondie asked scathingly. 'They 'ave lookouts on duty, twenty-four seven.'

'But we could get the guards first, knock them out and then put them in sacks so they can't escape.' Max's eyes shone with triumph.

Aysha folded her arms across her chest and gazed down at Max. 'Little boy, those guards are snowmen. They have powerful brooms and have been trained by ancient Chinese housewives in the martial art of Kleen Sweep. One swipe with a broom and you're done for.'

Max felt the glamorous dolls were not being very encouraging. 'We're not going to give up, are we, Ellie?'

Ellie shook her head, moved by Max's determination. Unfortunately she had no idea what they might be able to achieve. Everything in the Christmas Shop was so different from the world they knew.

'We'll think of something,' Max said hotly. 'Ellie and I will spy on them. We'll find out what the plan is and anything else useful too.'

'Fine,' muttered Blondie. 'By all means go an' get your arms an' legs blown off, or torn to bits by angels an' minced up.' She stalked off, followed by Aysha, swinging her crutch and dotting the floor as she went. Max and Ellie gazed after them.

'I don't like them,' pronounced Max. 'They just give up.'

'They've been fighting this war a lot longer than we have,' Ellie said. 'I guess it's pretty wearing and when you're tired you get cross and tetchy.'

'Like Mum?' Max suggested, making Ellie laugh. 'But we will go and spy on them, won't we?'

'It's going to be dangerous.'

'I'm not a baby!' cried Max.

'Of course not. But we've been shrunk. If we were big it would be easy, but we're titchy. We could easily get hurt.'

'I'm not scared!' Max declared.

'No, but I am,' Ellie admitted.

Max looked hard at his big sister, wondering if she was just pretending. His jaw jutted determinedly. 'It'll be OK,' he announced. 'And you can hold my hand.'

Once they had decided to become spies Ellie and Max found themselves being overwhelmed with information. The toys were eager to help and many had advice that they thought would be useful for Max and Ellie to know when they reached enemy territory on the far side of the

Empty Room – the big room where they had first landed.

'The angels always attack from the left side,' one penguin told them.

'Unless they attack from the right,' said another. 'I was attacked from the right once.'

The first penguin immediately faced him. 'You never have known your left from your right. Hold up your right flipper, go on.'

The second penguin lifted his right flipper.

'See?' cried the first penguin triumphantly. 'That's your left flipper. Look, this is my left

flipper, and you're holding up a flipper on the same side, so that's your left one.'

The second penguin shook his head. 'No, you're waving your right flipper at me. I'm holding up my right flipper, so you must be –'

'Come here, both of you,' ordered Ellie. She made the penguins stand beside each other and hold up their right flippers. She showed them how they were both doing the same thing. The two penguins began giggling and couldn't stop.

Dippy delivered his wise advice about different kinds of angels in slow, rumbling tones. 'The wooden-winged angels have nasty stings but they're slow. You can knock them out of the sky with your tail.'

Before Ellie could point out that neither she nor Max had tails the dinosaur gave a short and effective demonstration. He swished his tail high into the air, almost decapitating both the giraffes and sending a very surprised teddy flying right across the room. It came whumping down on a

whoopee cushion. *SPLRRRRGH!* At least it was a
soft landing.

'The ones with proper wings are fast,' Dippy
rumbled on. 'But you can dodge them by

zigzagging, I believe. It's not something I can do, personally speaking. Zigzagging isn't one of my talents, but smaller creatures can do it.'

'Thank you, Dippy,' smiled Ellie.

One of
the Three
Wise Men,
weighed
down by his
long, wispy
beard, tottered
up to the children.
'Lithen carefully,'
he couldn't help
lisping, as tufts of
beard got sucked into his mouth and stuck
between his teeth as he spoke. 'Whathever you
thoo, thon't go in thoo the Cupboard Under the
Thairth. Thereth a big monthter, a dangerwuth
monthter.'

The two commanders had returned and were
listening in. Aysha nodded seriously. 'Keep away
from it. When the cupboard door is shut all
is well. But if you open the door the monster
comes out and it is truly terrible. It is far more

dangerous than the Christmas Fairy and her angels.'

'We'll keep well clear of that, won't we, sis?' declared Max, eyes popping. His imagination had already stuffed the cupboard with a gigantic vampire dragon.

Ellie nodded, but her thoughts had moved on to another problem – how to avoid being captured. 'I've been thinking. The angels don't fight each other, do they?'

There was a loud chorus of surprised 'no's.

'Suppose Max and I disguise ourselves as angels? That way we won't have to sneak about. We can go anywhere we like.'

Blondie smiled at the others, flashing her perfect white teeth. 'What did I say? That girl is smart! OK, so she's come 'ere in 'er jim-jams, wiv no make-up and no 'andbag, but otherwise she is smart.'

It didn't take long for the toys to rustle up two pairs of wings. They had been cut out

of cardboard and cheerfully decorated by a
couple of small penguins with glitter and bits of
coloured paper. But there was a still a problem
– Max.

'Trouble is, he's not a girl,' Blondie said bluntly.
'All angels are girls.'

'The Angel Gabriel wasn't a girl,' Max
protested.

'Maybe, but all them angels on Christmas trees are girls, an' if they're not girls they certainly look girly because angels 'ave long dresses. You're in jeans,' Blondie continued relentlessly. 'You gotta wear a dress, Max.'

7 Superhero Max

'I am NOT wearing a dress!' Max said fiercely. His ears felt as if they were on fire.

Blondie calmly examined her hair for split ends. 'Either you wear a dress, or you get torn to shreds by angry angels. Hmm, fink I might change my shampoo.'

Max turned to Ellie but there was nothing she could do to help. Unfortunately Blondie was right. Ellie tried to comfort her brother. 'Think how brave you'll be.'

'It's not brave to wear a dress,' growled Max. 'It's STUPID!'

'You'll be saving Christmas for the world,' Ellie pointed out. 'You'll be a hero. Children across the world will think you're amazing.'

'Children across the world will laugh

themselves silly,' Max predicted.

'Dress or death?' asked Blondie.

It was a stark choice. Even Max could see that, and he caved in. 'Dress,' he mumbled at last. 'But it mustn't have frills or flowers or fiddly bits and everyone has to shut their eyes tight once I've got it on so they can't see how stupid I look.'

'OK,' smiled Ellie. 'Let's see if we can find a dress that fits.'

They hunted around and to their dismay they couldn't find one for Max. They were too big, too small or the wrong kind. There were several that suited Ellie, who was soon wearing a long white dress to hide her pyjamas, but Max was a problem. There was no suitable dress for him. He cheered up considerably.

'Bingo!' Blondie cried. 'Fink I 'ave just the fing.' The commander disappeared to her room for a couple of minutes and returned clutching a short white garment.

'It's my nightie,' she smirked. Max almost

choked on the spot.

'No way! I am NOT wearing a girly nightie! Ellie, please! Tell them! Look at it, Ellie – it's got feathery fluff stuff all round the bottom. I can't wear that. I am going to save Christmas for the world. It's not fair!'

But there was no alternative. It was the nightie or nothing. Max stamped his feet and said in that case he wasn't going to be a spy and he didn't care if Christmas never came again.

'You're such a fuss-face,' Blondie told him. 'We're fightin' a war an' all you can do is worry about wearin' a nightie. It don't bother me an' I wear it every night.'

'But you're a GIRL!' Max pointed out. 'Boys do NOT wear nighties, not even when there's a war.'

Ellie gently held Max's arm and pulled him away to a quiet corner. 'Max, I know it's really, really, really hard for you to do this but I need you with me. I can't do this on my own. None of

the others are coming. Only you can help me.'
They looked at each other for a long time, until
Max's eyes began to sting. He rubbed them hard
with his fists, walked quickly back to Blondie and
grabbed the wretched nightie from her.

'See?' began the commander. 'You –'

'Three cheers for Max!' cried Ellie, quickly
drowning out Blondie before she said something
that would throw Max back into a strop. Instead,
the room erupted with applause, which at least
brought a faint smile to Max's face. He stomped
off to a dark corner, angrily removed his jeans
and pulled the awful nightie over his head.

'I feel so stupid,' he mumbled to his sister as he
came back out.

'You look like a superhero,' Ellie told him,
suppressing the urge to laugh. 'And you *are* a
superhero,' she added.

'An' you've got such cute knees,' Blondie added
for good measure as she adjusted his wings. Max
glared back at her in silence.

Aysha checked both of them up and down
several times. This was a serious business. It was
vital that the enemy camp believed that Max and
Ellie were angels. Everyone became quiet. Some
of the toys wished the pair luck. They shook
hands, paws, flippers and wings.

Blondie took them to the sliding door. 'We'll

open it long enough to let you out. After that you're on your own. Good luck and goodbye.'

'That sounds a bit final,' Ellie murmured.

'Don't like goodbyes,' Blondie said gruffly, still examining them carefully to make sure the angelic details were correct. 'You're very brave, the pair of you. Make sure yous come back. Wait a sec, there's somefing missin'.' She sucked in her cheeks and studied their faces.

The blonde commander suddenly nodded. 'Make-up,' she declared, opening her silver clutch bag. Max was a deathly white. He stood stunned and speechless. First it was a nightie and now it was eyeliner. It couldn't get any worse.

'An' some red on those lovely chubby cheeks,' smiled Blondie, making a big red circle on each cheek. Max gritted his teeth and counted to ten to stop himself exploding.

'An' a nice dab of lippy.' Blondie deftly painted Max's mouth, while he counted to fifty. 'Perfect,' she declared.

'Now you really look angelic,' Aysha nodded.

'I want to die,' Max grunted.

'He doesn't really,' smiled Ellie, as Blondie began to work on her.

Max tried to regain his pride by asking if they could take weapons with them. He reckoned a tank would do nicely. At least it would hide the nasty nightie.

'I think the enemy might notice us in a tank,' laughed Ellie. 'But Max is right, we should have something.'

'It'll 'ave to be somefing the real angels might carry,' said Blondie. 'Like them long trumpets, but we ain't got no trumpets.'

'I've got my recorder,' Ellie remembered, tucking it into her belt.

'What about me?' asked Max.

'How about a crook from one of the shepherds in the nativity set?' Aysha suggested.

Max sighed and took the crook, glancing longingly back at the tank. It was time to go. There was no more to be said, just a few quick hugs and some more flipper shaking. The door opened. Max and Ellie stepped out into the dark and silent Empty Room beyond. The door behind them slid shut. For a brief second

the faulty Christmas lights sparked up and illuminated the No Man's Land ahead of them with an eerie mix of red, green, blue and yellow. They gave one last pathetic buzz and went off.

Ellie and Max were alone in the silent dark.

8 An Electrifying Task

'I don't like those pyjamas,' whispered Max as they skirted round the edge of the Empty Room. 'We're trapped in this stupid place and we might get killed by stupid angels with stupid wooden wings and nothing is real and we're titchy tiny and I look like a stupid girl and it's all the fault of those stupid pyjamas that Great-Aunt Stupid sent you.'

'I know,' admitted Ellie, who was feeling much the same herself.

'We've been shrunk, Ellie. We can't go back to our own world like this. We'll get trodden on by Dad for a start. His feet are as big as pizzas. And if Dad doesn't flatten us we'll be eaten by a spider or squeezed to death by a worm. We don't even know *how* to get back, do you?'

Ellie couldn't help noticing how Max had started with 'we' but finished it with 'you', as if it was all her fault. She swallowed an uncomfortable sense of guilt. She knew it wasn't like that really, but that was how she felt.

'I'm sorry,' she murmured, squeezing Max's hand. 'I promise we will get back and we will be the right size when we get home. After all, we didn't have to make ourselves shrink to get here, did we?'

Max stopped in his tracks. Even in the dark Ellie could see the smile creep on to his face. 'No! We didn't! It was like magic, wasn't it? That's what will happen when we go back!'

Now it was Max leading Ellie, as he happily marched forward. He even began to whistle until Ellie quickly told him to stop. They had reached enemy territory, on the far side of the Empty Room.

Blondie had pointed out an old electric plug socket, just above the skirting board. Plaster had crumbled away round one edge of the plastic plate and there was a big enough gap to wriggle through and get into the wall cavity. Once there they should find a crack they could squeeze through into the enemy camp next door.

However, nothing was going to be easy. They stood beneath the plastic socket, gazing up at it. Ellie nervously chewed her lower lip.

'There's no way to switch it off,' she confided, watching Max anxiously.

'Do you mean that everything inside is still electrified?' His sister nodded. 'So if it touches us,' Max went on, 'we will probably go BANG! and just be a puff of smoke?' Ellie nodded again. 'So we might DIE?' Max loved being dramatic.

Ellie held his hands. 'We are not going to die, Max. All we have to do is crawl past the wiring. I'll go first and you follow. If anything happens to me then you must go straight back to the others. Do you understand?'

'Yes,' nodded Max, suddenly becoming rather matter-of-fact about it all. 'But it won't do me any good if you get blown up because you're wearing the Cosmic Pyjamas, and if they get exploded all over the place I shall be stuck here for ever. In fact,' said Max emphatically, 'I'm going first.'

'But, Max —' Ellie began, only to be firmly interrupted.

'Crouch down so I can stand on your back,'

Max ordered. Ellie dropped to her hands and knees while Max hauled himself up to the thin top of the skirting board and stood there balancing like a mountaineer on a narrow ledge. He carefully lay down and reached towards his sister. She grabbed his hand, swung her legs on to the ledge and pulled herself up.

Max turned to the dark, jagged gap and without glancing back at Ellie he shouldered his way in. Crumbly lumps of plaster lay everywhere and soon their journey became a caving expedition. There was no room to stand and they were forced to crawl across scattered bits of brick and plaster which dug painfully into their knees.

They pressed forward and shortly they could see a writhing nest of thick coloured cables of wire curling in all directions, and an array of shiny brass screws, bars and plates. It was like being deep inside the belly of some fantastical beast.

They could also hear it. A low, growling hum

made everything seem to vibrate. Now and then
something would crackle noisily, sending sparks
snapping through the air like miniature lightning.

Ellie and Max had to find a path through all
this. They took off their wings so they wouldn't
catch on anything. They moved silently and
steadily among the deadly humming innards,
ducking their heads and clambering over bits of
cable. Sometimes they passed so close to a highly
charged piece of metal that their hair stood on
end. At last they dropped down into the wall cavity.

'We did it!' said Max, wearing a ridiculously large grin on his face.

'Well done! Here, let's get your wings back on. There's a crack in the wall over there. Maybe we can squeeze through.'

'What do we do when we get to the other side?' asked Max. It was a good question. They could hardly walk up to the nearest enemy angel and demand to know what the Dead Secret Plan was.

'We shall hang about,' Ellie said, a trifle lamely. 'We must keep our ears and eyes open and pick

up any useful information.'

'OK,' Max said cheerfully.
Hanging about would be a mere
trifle after braving the perils of
the plug socket.

They carefully pushed through
the crack and almost at once found themselves
in a very different set-up to
Blondie's hideout. Bright
lights and busy noise were
everywhere. It reminded
Ellie of being inside a
factory. Angels of all shapes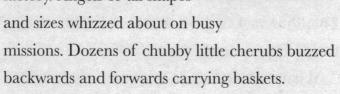
and sizes whizzed about on busy
missions. Dozens of chubby little cherubs buzzed
backwards and forwards carrying baskets.

'They're all coming and
going from that room at
the back,' Ellie observed.
'I'm sure they're doing
something in there. The

baskets going in have got something inside them, but the baskets coming out are empty. We must get in there and see.'

In one corner the Dove of Peace was surrounded by busy cherubs. Two donkeys, which Ellie immediately decided were the ones that had been kidnapped from the nativity sets, had been loaded up with what looked like small bombs. The donkeys carried their deadly cargo across to the Dove of Peace, where the cherubs busied themselves carefully loading the bombs into the Dove's bomb bay.

'That Christmas Fairy is totally twisted,' said Ellie. 'She is so evil. What kind of person would use a Dove of Peace to drop bombs?'

Max kept quiet. He was thinking what a neat idea it was, and could just see himself as a bomber pilot, homing in on the enemy to drop his giant splatter bombs.

Gangs of snowmen were toiling away on some kind of production line. At one end was a large, metal tower. Brightly coloured plastic containers, which Ellie quickly recognized as the plastic beakers that babies play with, were being piled high with a variety of ingredients. A toy crane hoisted the beakers to the top of the tower, where they were tipped inside. The tower throbbed and shook with a noisy chorus of gurgles, gulps, growls and the odd belch.

At the bottom of the tower squodgy yellow dollops were emerging on to a conveyor belt. As they passed along they were cut into sections by the snowmen and patted into shape before being placed in a basket. This was whisked away by a cherub and taken through to the back room.

No wonder this place reminded Ellie of a factory — it *was* a factory. But what was it making? A pungent smell hung in the air and it reminded Ellie of something. She kept thinking of nuts, but that didn't make any sense. What would the angels want with nuts? Were they planning to mow down Blondie's army of penguins by rolling hazelnuts at them? Were they building a giant cannon that fired pecans and brazils?

A loud clatter came from above them and a large, rotund angel with wooden wings landed right beside them, quickly followed by a second, even tubbier, one.

'What do you think you're doing?' demanded the first. The second had hardly folded her wings before she began picking her nose as if she'd just found gold up her nostril.

Max and Ellie had been discovered.

9 The Cupboard Under the Stairs

'Pardon?' answered Ellie, trying to gain some thinking time.

'I said, what's up with you? Why aren't you flying?'

'Um, I got a wing injury in the last battle,' Ellie invented madly.

The fatter angel pulled a face. 'Ooh, painful. What you should do, love, is stay at the back. That's what Flora here and I do when there's an attack going on. We stay at the back and have a little chat. Hide behind the others, love, like we do. Then you don't get hit, see?'

'Yes,' Ellie agreed.

Flora was peering at Max. 'What's wrong with her then? She been hit too?'

Max's little face flushed angrily. 'I'm not a

gir–' he began, as Ellie hastily clamped a hand over his mouth.

'No, she's all right,' Ellie said quickly. 'She's looking after me.'

'Oh? I thought Her Right Royal Pain-In-The-Bumtiddly-Diddly-Department, if you get my meaning, ordered everyone to work on the Dead Secret Plan?'

'That's right,' agreed Ellie. 'But I can't fly and to tell you the truth, my little friend here, Nettle, keeps dropping things. Christmas Fairy says she's more of a nuisance than a help.'

Flora and her friend sniggered. 'That's a good trick! We must try that one, love. That'd get us out of all this bloomin' work. Treats us like slaves, she does.' Flora lifted the corner of her dress to scratch a wooden leg. 'Got a splinter,' she confided.

'Not nice,' said Ellie. 'Do you think you should get back before the Right Royal Pain notices?'

'Oh, I suppose so.' Flora turned to Max and

patted him on the head. 'By the way, I love your
dress.'

'You can have it if you want,' Max said,
through gritted teeth.

'So kind – a proper little angel, you are, but it'd
be much too small for me.'

Now it was the other angel's turn to admire
Max. 'Bye, Nettle. I love your name, by the way.
It's got a nice ring to it.'

'More like a nice sting to it!' chortled Flora,

and her shoulders began to heave with laughter. 'Now then, time flies, and so must we. Cheery-bye!'

Max and Ellie watched them climb slowly towards the ceiling to join the others, flapping their cumbersome wings. Ellie couldn't help feeling pleased with herself and she grinned at her brother.

'They thought we were proper angels,' she said.

'You called me Nettle,' bristled Max.

'And you nearly gave us away,' Ellie retorted. 'I had to think quickly.' She glanced towards the room at the back. 'We must get in there.'

'How are we going to do that?'

'Everyone thinks we're angels. Maybe we can walk straight in. We'll pick up a basket like the cherubs and carry that with us. Hopefully everyone will think we're helping.'

They walked calmly across to the end of the conveyor belt. They nodded towards the snowmen and each picked up a basket. Nobody questioned or stopped them. They headed for the room at the back, with Ellie whispering excitedly to Max. 'Do you know what this stuff is that we're carrying?'

'Yes. It's stinky-poo stuff.' Max was holding his nose. 'We should stick it in the nearest dustbin.'

'The smell comes from almonds. I reckon they're making marzipan.'

'Urgh!' choked Max, his nose wrinkling in disgust. 'I knew it was something horrible.' He gazed back at the tin tower. 'You mean the angels are making marzipan in that tower? Why do they want so much of it?'

Ellie shrugged and hoped that they would soon find out. They reached the entrance to the back room. It was heavily guarded by large, beefy snowmen wielding stiff brooms.

'What have you got there?' demanded one. As he spoke his plastic carrot nose fell off. He picked it up and stabbed it back into place the wrong

way round, grumbling about the lack of quality control. Ellie held up her basket for the snowman to inspect.

'All right, pass,' ordered the snowman and the children walked through. It was that easy! They exchanged brief smiles and turned to study the mystery room.

It was awesome. They were at the heart of the Dead Secret Plan. Angels and snowmen whizzed about attending to a hundred different jobs:

fetching, carrying, building and moulding.

Marzipan was everywhere, but even so, there was one thing that grabbed Ellie and Max's attention more than anything else. A towering network of scaffolding made from a multicoloured plastic kit had been constructed to support the angels' building work, and what they were building was a giant.

A GIANT MAN, MADE OF MARZIPAN.

'He's huge!' cried Max.

'Yesss,' hissed a familiar voice. 'Marzipan Man is almost finished.'

It was the Christmas Fairy herself, who hadn't recognized them. She stood next to Ellie and Max, admiring the monster-man she had created and at the same time she twisted and jerked and scratched her rear with thin fingers.

'Once we get Marzipan Man going nobody will be able to stop him – except me!'

'Really?' prompted Ellie.

'Oh, yesss! Marzipan Man will crush

everything in his path. Those ridiculous glamour-dolls will be able to do nothing.' The Christmas Fairy suddenly did a surprisingly good imitation of Blondie. 'Don't you come no closer, Marzipan Man, or I shall paint your toenails red! Oh, oh, please don't 'urt me, you might spoil my lipstick!'

The Christmas Fairy pulled such a disgusted smirk that her one eye almost fell out. 'Pah! She is so pathetic! With his Mega-Marzipanator my monster creation will be able to sssmother everything with hundreds of tons of marzipan.'

'That's revolting!' groaned Max. He'd never liked marzipan in the first place.

The Christmas Fairy rubbed her hands with glee. 'And when Father Christmas walks in here, won't he be sssurprised? He will be marzipanned from head to toe and that will be the end of him, and of Christmasss. For ever. Ha ha ha ha ha!'

The Christmas Fairy chortled with glee and grinned fiercely at her two small companions. A tiny gleam of recognition crept into her eyes. A bony hand shot out and grasped Ellie's shoulder.

'Do I know you? Have we met before?'

'I don't think so,' replied Ellie as calmly as she could considering the Fairy's sharp nails were beginning to claw her painfully.

'Oh yesss, let me sssee, we'll just wipe off some

of this make-up and goodness me, if it isn't my old friends, the mince ssspiesss!'

The Christmas Fairy grabbed at Ellie's angel dress and lifted it up. 'Yesss! You're ssstill wearing those peculiar pyjamas too. You can take off those ridiculous wingsss and that dress at once! And you too!' ordered the Christmas Fairy, glaring at Max.

Suddenly Max found himself in the wholly unexpected position of wanting to keep his awful nightie *on*. He clutched it to his chest and tried to pull it down to his knees. The Christmas Fairy broke into an hysterical cackle.

'The boy wants his nightie! There, there, it's all right, my little sssweety-pie, you can keep your precious pretty thing.' Her beady eye spun round and fixed on Ellie's recorder, tucked into her belt. 'What's that?' she demanded suspiciously.

'This?' asked Ellie, seizing the opportunity for a bit of trickery. 'It's a very powerful weapon. You'd better watch out.' Ellie reached for her recorder but the Christmas Fairy shot out a gnarled hand and gripped her wrist.

'Oh no, you don't,' she hissed, giving Ellie a toothless grin. 'I'll take that.' She pulled the recorder from Ellie's belt and examined it. 'There's a sssimple way to deal with thisss,' the Christmas Fairy went on, and before Ellie could say another word the wicked hag broke the recorder across her knee, snapping it in half.

Max goggled at the Christmas Fairy, horrified. 'You are going to be in such big trouble with Mrs Tompkinson,' he told her.

'Oh, I am ssso ssscared,' spat the Christmas Fairy, throwing away the broken instrument. Her wrinkled, grey hands darted out and she grabbed each of the children by one ear.

'You have done well to get this far,' she sneered unpleasantly, 'but now you are my prisoners. Guardsss, take these mince ssspiesss away and put them in the dungeon.'

A gasp of horror went through everyone. The angels stopped work, hovering in mid air. 'The dungeon?' they repeated. Even the guards were aghast.

'Your Highness, do you really mean the dungeon?'

'Yes! Of course I do!' she snapped.

'The one with the monster in it?'

'Yesss, yesss, yesss!' roared the Christmas Fairy.

102

'Get on with it! Put them in THE CUPBOARD UNDER THE STAIRSSS!'

The entire room looked on almost in pity as Max and Ellie were dragged away. Under a large guard of snowmen and heavily armed fairies the two children were marched out to the Empty Room and taken across to the stair cupboard. The door was briefly opened, the children were shoved into the darkness and the door slammed tight shut behind them. The sound of marching feet died away and they were left on their own.

10   The Secret Pocket

It was utterly dark at first. It seemed to take an age for their eyes to get used to it and all that time Ellie and Max hardly dared breathe, let alone move. They stood in silence, ears pricked, trying to pick out the sounds of any approaching beast.

Max's hand crept into Ellie's, or maybe it was the other way round. At last the light seeping in beneath the door began to reveal the inside of the cupboard. They could make out some of the gigantic shapes around them, objects that both Max and Ellie quickly recognized from their own stair cupboard at home. Beside a mop and bucket, a vacuum cleaner stood tall and threatening. The machine loomed over them.

At last Max had to open his mouth. 'What

monster do you think is in here?' he whispered.

'I don't know,' Ellie whispered back. 'Mice? Rats?'

Max was grasping his shepherd's crook tightly. Ellie was feeling exhausted by all the excitement, not to mention the awful disappointment of

being captured. They had gathered hugely
important information about the Dead Secret
Plan but had no chance now of getting it to
Blondie and Aysha. She dragged some old dusters
together to make a pile to sleep on but when she
lay down it was lumpy and uncomfortable.

Ellie lifted a bit of duster and felt around.
Her hand touched something hard. Lifting the
duster a bit more she reached in and pulled out
something long and slim. It was a plastic leg. The
children examined it with curious horror.

'I think this is Aysha's missing leg,' Ellie
whispered.

'Yuck,' muttered Max. 'How did it get in here?'

'I have no idea,' said Ellie. 'And I'm too tired to think about it now. I've got to have a sleep, a quick nap. You stay on guard. Wake me if anything happens or if you get scared.'

Max puffed out his chest. 'I won't get scared,' he said, but Ellie was already asleep. Max was as good as his word. He didn't get scared, but that might have been because within five minutes he was fast asleep too.

Three or four hours passed before they woke. Nothing had changed. It was still dark. More importantly, no monsters had appeared, which surprised both of them and got Ellie thinking.

'Max, suppose the monster in the cupboard isn't a monster at all?'

Max looked at his big sister pityingly. 'Monsters are monsters, Ellie. They can't *not* be monsters. If they weren't monsters they wouldn't *be* monsters, would they?'

Max's perfect logic didn't change what Ellie was thinking. She pointed at the vacuum cleaner. 'What's that?' she asked Max.

'A vacuum cleaner.'

'Let's call it a monster instead.'

'It's a vacuum cleaner,' repeated Max.

'Suppose the Christmas Fairy and her angels don't call it that? Maybe they don't know it's a vacuum cleaner. Suppose they think it's a monster? The vacuum cleaner doesn't bother us because we know what it is, but maybe the others don't. I think that all the toys here – Blondie, Aysha, the Christmas Fairy, everyone – they all think that it's a monster. Max, we're not in danger. We are completely safe!'

'Wow! That's a relief,' said Max, his eyes popping. Then his shoulders slumped. 'But we're still shut inside.'

'Maybe we can find a way out, or a way of opening the door.'

Max gazed up at the handle, far above them.

There was no way they could reach it. Ellie was determined though.

'We have to escape. You heard what the Christmas Fairy said – Marzipan Man is almost complete, and Father Christmas could arrive at any time.'

Max was cheesed off. Everything was so up and down. One moment they'd be facing death and the next moment the monster wasn't a monster at all and just when they were getting excited about that they'd discover some other awful problem. 'I wish we'd never seen those Cosmic Pyjamas,' he said.

Ellie sat down beside him. 'I know. It must be almost Christmas and we're still stuck here.'

'When we get back home I'm going to burn them,' Max declared.

Ellie's new nightwear had certainly caused a lot of trouble but on the other hand there was something so weirdly mysterious about them that she was both enchanted and repelled.

Ellie gazed at the puzzling pyjamas in the gloom of the cupboard. Sometimes she thought that each little picture seemed to be part of a story, maybe even trying to tell a story. Ellie found herself wondering if another picture might start quivering, might 'come alive', just as the Christmas Shop had, and if it did, what might happen. But there was no trembling picture to save them.

Instead, Ellie spotted what at first she thought was a worm, or a snake. It seemed to be slithering *between* all the little pictures. It was difficult to see properly in the gloom. She bent her head close to her sleeve, peering intently, then suddenly she jerked up. It wasn't a worm or a snake. It was a message. And the message said:

LOOK IN THE POCKET.

Ellie was about to show Max when the

message slowly vanished, right in front of her eyes. She had seen it for such a short time she began to wonder if she had ever seen it at all, but of course she had.

What pocket was she supposed to look in? The pyjamas didn't have a pocket. On the other hand a few moments ago her pyjamas hadn't had a wriggling message either.

Ellie began to pat the pyjamas all over, running her hands down her arms and legs. There was an odd ridge under the material near her left ankle. She lifted her foot and felt around.

A pocket. A small pocket on the *inside* leg of her pyjamas, down near her heel. Had it always been there? Ellie didn't think so, it was such a crazy place to find a pocket. She had to roll up the leg to get at it, and when she dabbled two fingers inside she immediately felt something.

It was a small tube. Now she was certain it had never been there before. Ellie silently showed Max the little tube, and he almost screamed with excitement.

'It says DYNAMITE on this!'

Ellie nodded dumbly, too fearful to speak. Max was almost jumping with excitement.

'Wow! Dynamite! Where did you get it from?'

Ellie told him about the message and the pocket.

'How come you never noticed before?' demanded Max.

'The message wasn't there and neither was the pocket. They've only just arrived.'

'That's daft,' Max said bluntly, which made Ellie smile.

'I know, it's crazy. These pyjamas are kind of spooky.'

'Well, I think they're more like stupid pyjamas,' said Max, warming to his old theme. 'Nobody puts dynamite in their pyjama pocket. Where is the pocket anyway? Show me.'

Ellie rolled up her pyjama leg. The pocket

was no longer there.

'But that's impossible,' Max complained.

Ellie shrugged. 'Great-Aunt Jemima said that these are Cosmic Pyjamas. Maybe Cosmic Pyjamas do impossible things. After all, it was the pyjamas that brought us here and that was pretty strange, wasn't it?'

Max was still studying the little stick of dynamite. 'What does "ignitting" mean?'

Ellie shrugged. 'Why?'

'There's very small writing round the top of

the tube. It says "self-ignitting". Look.' Max passed the dynamite back to his sister who almost screamed and dropped the tube to the floor.

'SELF-IGNITING, Max! Not ignitting. Igniting. That means it goes off by itself!'

The two children gazed in horror at the tube, gently rolling backwards and forwards between their feet. They wanted to run, but where can you run when you're stuck in a cupboard?

It was Max who asked the obvious. 'So when's it going to explode?'

'How should I know?' Ellie snapped.

'Keep your knickers on,' grunted Max tetchily.

'That's exactly what I would like to do,' Ellie shot back. 'I would very much like not to have my knickers blown right off, thank you very much.'

Max sniggered. 'That's funny.'

'Oh, ha ha. You won't be laughing when we

both get blown up.' Ellie began to gingerly push the dynamite across the floor with one foot. Max asked her what she was doing.

'If we put this dynamite under the edge of the door in the corner it might make enough of a hole for us to crawl out.'

'Suppose the Christmas Fairy hears the explosion?' asked Max.

'Suppose she doesn't? Even better, Max, suppose my plan works and we manage to escape? Anyhow, it might not go off at all.'

Max gave in with a shrug. 'OK,' he said. It was one of the things Ellie loved about her little brother. He was never cross with her for long.

Ellie still could not bring herself to pick up the dynamite but she eventually managed to roll it to the far corner of the door. Max went and hid beneath the dusters.

'I'll put it under the door, dash back to you and wait,' said Ellie. 'Get ready to make your escape. If anything goes wrong and we get separated, make your way back to Blondie.'

Max didn't answer. He was not planning on getting separated from his sister under any circumstances. Ellie raced across to Max and dived beneath the dusters.

'Ow!' squealed Max. 'Gerroff, you great pudding. Gerroff!'

'Do shut up, Max. Do you think the dynamite will know we want it to go off?'

Max pulled back the duster a fraction and yelled, 'You can blow up now!'

'Max, you're talking to a stick of dynamite,' giggled Ellie.

'So what?' he shrugged. 'We've been shrunk. We've got pyjamas with disappearing pockets and weird pictures. We've been talking to Barbie dolls and Christmas fairies and plastic dinosaurs and now you think it's crazy to talk to a stick of dynamite. Ellie, this whole world we're in is crazy.'

'Maybe, but that dynamite hasn't exploded yet. Let's do a countdown. Five, four, three –'

BOOOOOMMMMM!!!!!

Everything in the cupboard rattled like mad and the mop handle toppled forward against the door as if it had been fatally wounded. The children poked their heads out into a minor storm of whirling dust and scraps of paper. They hurried across to the corner of the door and discovered to their delight that the explosion had dislodged a large chunk of doorframe. Ellie gazed at the shattered frame.

'Oh well, now we know that dynamite sticks can't count. I only got to three. But it worked! Brilliant! Come on!'

They scrambled through, Max struggling with Aysha's missing leg. Ellie's eyes boggled. 'Why have you got that ghastly thing with you?' she wanted to know.

'I'm taking it back for Aysha,' Max said simply. 'Maybe she can put it back on.'

A single angel spy came swooping down to see what was going on, alerted by the explosion. Grasping the leg firmly round the ankle, as if it were a baseball bat, Max gave an almighty swing and BAM! The angel was sent spinning and unconscious right across the room. It clattered into a dark corner and lay still and silent.

'That sorts that out,' Max muttered grimly. 'Come on!'

They raced across the dark floor of the Empty Room, and arrived, panting but safe, beside the skirting board on the far side. They hammered at the sliding door.

'Let us in!' they yelled. 'Let us in! Hurry!'

11 Let Battle Begin!

'Didn't think you'd make it,' said Blondie, shaking her head. Aysha stared at Max in disbelief. He stood, grinning from ear to ear, with the commander's missing leg resting over one shoulder

'Darling child,' she cried. 'Where did you find it?'

This was Max's moment. He struck a casually heroic pose. 'Oh,' he began, 'it was in the cupboard under the stairs.'

'THE CUPBOARD UNDER THE STAIRS??!!' The whole room shrieked in dismay.

'Yes,' confirmed Max. 'It was just lying there, so we brought it back with us.'

'You tellin' me yous been in the Cupboard Under the Stairs?' asked Blondie, while Aysha took her leg from Max and examined it for damage. She let her colouring-pencil crutch drop to the floor and carefully slotted her leg back in place.

'My dear boy, I shall be grateful to you for the rest of my life. You have been so brave.'

'Nah,' said Max, with a shake of his head.
'Like I said, it was just lying there so I took it.'
But he couldn't play at being Mr Cool for long
and at last his excitement overcame him. He gave
a wild whoop and performed several forward
rolls, greatly admired by the penguins.

'We can only roll sideways,' confided one.

'Did you find out anyfing?' Blondie wanted to
know. 'What are them angels up to?'

'Let me sit down first,' said Ellie, slowly getting
her breath back. While Max hastily rid himself
of the hated nightie and reclaimed his jeans, Ellie
began to relate everything that had happened.

As she described Marzipan Man and his Mega-Marzipanator a dense cloud of gloom slowly descended upon the camp.

'How tall would you say Marzipan Man is?' Aysha asked.

'Same size as a proper human.'

The two commanders glanced at each other and quickly turned their eyes away. Each could see only one outcome to this – defeat. How could they possibly battle against such a giant, especially one that was able to cover everything in sight with one blast of his Marzipanator?

'An' you say Marzipan Man is almost complete?' Blondie murmured.

Ellie nodded. She couldn't think of anything to say. She kept digging into her brain, trying to think of something that might help, some way of attacking Marzipan Man. If only they had a flame-thrower or something similar. But then of course a flame-thrower that was small enough for them to handle would be useless against

Marzipan Man. It would be like holding a match to his big toe. They would need a giant flame-thrower.

''Ang on a sec,' Blondie began with a startled squeak. 'Them jimmy-jams of yours are doin' somefing weird. Look.'

The two commanders and Max gathered round Ellie and stared at where Blondie was pointing. Another message had appeared, wriggling across Ellie's right shoulder.

LET MONSTER FIGHT MONSTER.

That was all.

'Let monster fight monster?' murmured Aysha. 'What does that mean?'

'Marzipan Man is a monster,' grunted Blondie, and Ellie's face lit up.

'That's it! We have to find a monster to fight a monster, a monster that can defeat Marzipan Man.'

'Don't 'ave no monsters,' grumbled Blondie. 'Your jimmy-jams are a fat lot of use. That's the trouble wiv stuff that ain't designer, see? Know my clutch bag? Genuine Versace, that is, an' everyone, I mean everyone, notices it. Makes 'em squeal with envy. Nobody ain't gonna squeal at your jimmy-jams.'

Ellie waited patiently until the commander had finished criticizing her pyjamas and then quietly pointed out that they *did* have a monster that could fight Marzipan Man.

'Yeah, right,' snorted Blondie. 'If you mean Dippy the diplodocus, he's useless.'

'Thank you,' sighed the dinosaur, poking his head over the top of them all.

'No offence, Dippy, but you ain't monster enough to fight some bloomin' ginormous Marzipan Man, are you?' The dinosaur shook his head sadly.

Aysha put a hand on Blondie's shoulder. 'I think we should listen to Ellie. She has a plan.

125

Let her tell us what it is, Blondie, and stop
interrupting the poor girl.'

Ellie smiled at her gratefully and went on. 'The
idea is simple, but carrying it out will be difficult,'
Ellie began. 'We need to open the door to the
Cupboard Under the Stairs —', she began only to
be drowned out by more howls of dismay.

'THE CUPBOARD UNDER THE STAIRS?
Are you crazy?'

'Do you want to kill us all?'

'I don't want to die! Not the night before
Christmas!'

Ellie calmly waited until the protests had
died down before she continued. 'We use the
cupboard monster to fight Marzipan Man. The
monster in that cupboard isn't a monster at all.
It's a machine that can be switched on and off.
Remember, Max and I were in that cupboard
for a long time and we came to no harm. The
angels certainly won't expect to be attacked by a
monster. If we can get it out of the cupboard we

could use the vacuum cleaner. We also need to be able to switch it on.'

'It'll be brilliant!' declared Max, his eyes shining with excitement.

Blondie, Aysha, the penguins, the Marys and Josephs, the dinosaurs and teddies – in fact everyone else – looked aghast.

'You want to release the monster from the Cupboard Under the Stairs?' Aysha repeated.

'Listen, we can control it. It has an on–off switch just like every electrical machine. In the world Max and I come from we use vacuum cleaners every day – at least our mum and dad do. It might seem like a monster to you, but it's perfectly tame as long as we control it. We have little time left. We need to –'

Blondie stepped in. She was still the commander.

'Ellie's way too smart for us, an' she's right. We need to act fast. I want everyone 'ere to tool up for a final battle wiv the Christmas Fairy and her army. I also want all of you to put your 'eads together an' fink of 'ow we can open the door to the Cupboard Under the Stairs. 'Ow will we get the vacuum monster out? 'Ow do we plug it into a socket? 'Ow do we switch it on? I want answers, now.'

The toys began to bustle about, talking excitedly. A few remained full of doom and gloom.

'We're all going to die,' muttered a camel.

'It will never work,' said a shepherd.

'We're going to be marzipanned,' the camel continued,

before mournfully asking the shepherd what marzipan actually was. 'It's obviously something very nasty, maybe something plasticky. I don't like plastic at all and, no offence towards our dear plastic commanders, but I always think it's a bit, well, tacky, don't you?'

But for every complainer there were at least ten toys racking their brains. Slowly, bit by bit, suggestions came in to HQ. Aysha, Blondie, Max and Ellie listened carefully to each one. Some were immediately dismissed as unworkable, some were kept for further discussion and some were put into effect at once.

So it was that Ellie climbed into a large metal crane-truck and motored to the sliding door. She drove across the Empty Room and reached the cupboard without incident. Ellie began to raise the arm of the crane. The idea was simple. The crane would lift a heavy weight and hang it on the handle of the door. Ellie hoped the weight would pull the handle down and release the door.

It took her a few moments to learn how to control the arm of the crane but she soon got the hang of it and she raised the arm to its greatest height. It was immediately obvious that the crane was not tall enough. The first idea had failed.

Ellie lowered the lifting arm and as she did so two wooden-winged angels buzzed close by. She had been spotted. The angels banged off a couple of stings, which bounced harmlessly off the metal truck. Then they hurried away to report back to the Christmas Fairy. Now the Christmas Fairy would marshal her troops and they would surely attack, and Ellie had not even managed to open the cupboard door yet.

Blondie's army was already in big trouble.

12 The Battle Rages

'Plan B,' announced Ellie, back at the camp. 'And as quick as you can. Max, I'm sorry. The crane didn't work. It's down to you.'

Ellie had hoped to avoid Plan B, which was a lot more dangerous than Plan A. It meant using the fire engine and its long extending ladder to climb up to the door handle. The problem was that Ellie was too big to climb the ladder. It would have to be Max. More worryingly, it left Max exposed to all the angels as he climbed. He would have to wear a protective layer of armour, which would make climbing awkward, to say the least. Ellie felt guilty about making Max take on this dangerous task, but there was no other option.

They hunted around for some kind of armour

and eventually a stegosaurus nosed out a pile of pin-on badges. They had Christmas messages written on them. One said: CHRISTMAS IS COMING! Another said: I HATE XMAS PUDDING! There were many more. It was a struggle fixing them on, but at last Max was reasonably well sting-proofed. The penguins then helped themselves to the badge pile. They were going to use them as shields.

They got the fire engine out and Max clattered on board, his badges banging together. Now they needed to get to the Cupboard Under the Stairs as quickly as possible, before the angels could mount an attack. The door slid open, Ellie put her foot on the gas and the fire engine shot across the Empty Room with the penguins waddling behind as fast as they could to catch up.

Max climbed on to the ladder clutching a coil of string with a small weight on one end. As the ladder began to lift and extend he was carried higher and higher and he paid out the string so that one end remained on the ground, held fast by a large group of penguins. At last Max reached the door handle, and there was no sign of the angels – yet.

Max slipped the weighted end of the string over the handle and allowed it to lower itself to the ground. Here it was immediately gathered in by some penguins and they passed it round the heavy weight that had been left behind when the crane attempt was abandoned. The main group now hauled on the other end of the string, while Max began his descent.

The weight slowly rose from the ground and pulled down the door handle. With a faint click the door opened a fraction. A triumphant cheer went up from the penguins and they began to stream towards the opening. At that very same moment the angels launched their attack.

They came screaming down from above, wave after wave, scattering the penguins in every direction. The weight came crashing back down,

missing
the fire
engine by a
mere fraction.
Stings began to
zing past Max's
ears and thud into
the woodwork behind
him. Many pinged off
his armour, but some got
through, finding gaps here
and there and piercing
the backs of his legs and
arms. He tried not to cry
out, but sometimes he couldn't
help himself. It was as if he was
surrounded by angry wasps.

Max almost fell down the last section of ladder before throwing himself into the shelter of the driver's cab. Ellie flung her arms round him, squeezing him tightly before doing a sharp reverse away from the door. They raced straight back to the safety of the camp.

In the meantime the penguins were bravely trying to regroup and hold off the angel attack, but with little success. Reinforcements were needed and Blondie and Aysha rolled out in their tanks. This was better! Angels began to tumble from the sky as the tanks pounded them with hundreds and thousands.

It was clear that a massive battle had begun, and it was going to be decisive. It was win or lose, Christmas or no Christmas ever again. And Father Christmas himself was due to arrive at any moment. Ellie and Max *had* to get into the Cupboard Under the Stairs.

The angel commanders were quick to see that they were being overpowered by the two tanks and immediately sent for their own. They arrived with an enormous rumbling noise – not two, but four tanks, bigger and more powerful than Blondie's. The Christmas Fairy's tanks didn't deal with piddling little ammunition such as hundreds and thousands. They were loaded with the heavy silver, red and green balls that went on fairy cakes. It was fairy ammunition, and it was devastating.

Penguins were blasted to bits, sending splinters of plastic flying through the air. Then the biggest of the Christmas Fairy's tanks turned its sights on Blondie and Aysha. The new tank was fearsome, capable of firing off round after round of whole jellybeans.

Blondie's tank was pounded so hard that it spun round and faced backwards. She struggled to regain control but she was a sitting duck. The next round hit her broadside and toppled the tank on to its side. Blondie scrambled out, quickly followed by her crew of three choirboys. They

fled for safety, covered by the brave penguins.

Back at the camp the injured fighters were being brought back for treatment. A quiet, efficient team of Marys saw to their needs and patched them up as best they could. Many of them staggered back out to continue fighting.

They were trying to save Christmas for The
World.

Aysha's tank turret got a direct jellybean hit
and burst into flames. Having only just reached
the shelter of the camp, Ellie and Max dashed
straight back out in the fire engine. They

zigzagged around falling debris and injured fighters before screeching to a halt beside the stricken tank. Aysha was still inside, trapped by the flames. Ellie ran out the hose while Max started the water pumps. They were easy targets for the buzzing angels and they both came under a barrage of stings.

Blondie sent out a large force of shepherds to help. They had been specially trained and now they used their extra-long shepherds' crooks to great effect. They whirled and swirled them in the air, catching angels that dared to fly too low and knocking them out of the sky. It gave Ellie and Max just enough of a break to drag Aysha from the burning tank and carry her to the safety of the camp.

Blondie bent over her friend anxiously, but Ellie quickly reassured her that she was just a bit concussed and would recover. Blondie was relieved but not happy.

'My scouts 'ave reported that Father Christmas's sleigh 'as landed. 'E'll come walkin' through that front door any minute.'

'We can't delay any longer,' muttered Ellie. 'We have to get inside the cupboard. It's our only chance. Is the crack team ready?'

Blondie nodded and called them over. They were more of a motley bunch than a crack team, but there had been little time to train them. The ever-loyal penguins eagerly huddled together. Several elephants, camels, hippos and rhinoceroses had been drafted in from a collection of arks. Hopefully they knew what they had to do, and the first thing was to get across to the Cupboard Under the Stairs, on the far side of the Empty Room. Ellie peeped out at the raging battle ahead of them.

Blondie shook her head. 'You ain't finkin' of goin' out there an' just wanderin' across to that cupboard, are you? You'll be spifflicated, girl! I've got a better idea. Let's get some steam up!' The commander nodded towards a large tin train with several carriages. 'Climb on board. You're goin' for the ride of your life!'

They would make a dash for it, as simple as that. The troops boarded the train, which waited patiently as far back from the sliding door as possible, building up a head of steam. It would need as much speed as possible before heading into the battle. The last passenger to board was Dippy, crouching down as best he could in an open wagon at the rear.

The train sat there, huffing, puffing – quietly

quivering with power. Max and Ellie climbed into the driver's cab. Blondie stood by the sliding door and gave the signal. The brakes were released. The wheels spun furiously, striking sparks from the floor and then the train began to surge forward, straight for the door. At the last moment Blondie's penguins slid back the door and the train burst out into the midst of the battle, heading straight for the wall immediately next to the cupboard door.

Fighting warriors threw themselves out of the engine's storming path. The Christmas Fairy's tanks immediately tried to get their sights fixed on the speeding juggernaut. Jellybeans exploded around the train, spurting up from the ground in great clouds of sugar and splintered candy. The Dove of Peace swooped over several times, dropping her payload of splatter bombs, but so far the train had escaped damage.

It reached the far side of the Empty Room and began to slow. It was still going much too

fast to avoid a collision, but it allowed the crack team to fling themselves from the carriages. They tumbled and rolled across the ground, picked themselves up, ran for the open cupboard door and sheltered inside.

Meanwhile the train, with only Dippy still on board in the last carriage, thundered headlong into the wall. With a screech of tortured tin, the carriages were shunted on top of one another,

piling up into a mountain of mangled metal.
Wheels twisted off their axles and rolled away.
The final wagon toppled over on its side.

Dippy took one glance behind at the chaos that
surrounded him and hurried into the cupboard.
Together, the toys put their backs to the door and
pushed. Slowly the door swung wide open.

Ellie was delighted. Not only had they got the
door open but the effect it had on the Christmas

Fairy's troops was electric. Half of them fled in terror, thinking that they were about to be overwhelmed by a monster from the depths of the cupboard.

Ellie and her troops whooped and cheered in triumph, but the Christmas Fairy had not lost the battle by any means. Her answer was simple and devastating. The door to the rebel camp was thrown open and there stood – MARZIPAN MAN!

13 Marzipanned!

He was huge. He was vast, and he was marzipan from top to toe. He towered above everything, staring down with his sugar lozenge eyes at the tiny warriors fighting their tiny battle. Inside his massive body hundreds of snowmen toiled away to make him move. He stepped forward, rocking slightly. Behind him masses of snowmen with brooms came marching, ready to finally sweep the floor clear of the enemy.

Marzipan Man raised the Mega-Marzipanator, and pulled the trigger.

SPLURRRPPP!!!

A giant stream of marzipan squirted out of the barrel and smacked down on a group of penguins, smearing them against the floor. With every step that Marzipan Man took the floor

shuddered. Now he slowly turned to face the Cupboard Under the Stairs. Once again he raised his gun and –

SPLURRRPPPP!

This time a great dollop splattered down by the doorframe. Sitting astride an elephant, Ellie turned to her troops.

'Get that electric plug in! Get that tube out!'

The penguins seized the electric plug and carried it above their heads to the nearest socket. Carefully they got the three metal prongs ready to slide into the socket. This was Dippy's moment. Unmoved by the stings that the angels showered down on him, he swung his tail back as far he could and then, with a great THWACK!! he whipped his tail round and rammed the plug fairly and squarely into the socket.

Meanwhile a second group of penguins, teddy bears, camels and elephants struggled to bring out the vacuum cleaner hose. They stood at the ready, waiting for Ellie's command.

SPLURRRPPP-A-DURRRPPP!!!!

Marzipan Man had just marzipanned half the plug-penguins, splattering them against the skirting board. He swung his Mega-Marzipanator towards Ellie and the tube gang.

'Switch on, Max!' yelled Ellie. 'Now!'

Inside the cupboard, Max was ready. He had managed to clamber halfway up the side of the vacuum cleaner, along with Blondie and Aysha, and now the three of them were balanced on a large plastic clip. The trio would only get one chance to get this right. They held hands and Max counted down.

'Three, two, one, JUMP!'

Still holding hands, the three friends leaped into the air. They fell rapidly, faster and faster until KER-THUMPP! They landed slap-bang on the power button.

The vacuum cleaner roared into life and the tube was almost ripped out of Ellie's grasp as she and the penguins struggled to control it.

'Tube holders – forward march!' cried Ellie, from her elephant, and they began to carry the air-swallowing monster straight towards Marzipan Man.

SPLURRRPPP!

A great splat of marzipan thudded down right beside them, knocking one or two of the tube gang off their feet. More penguins came hurrying over to replace them. Bit by bit the tube moved forward. A great wind was now sucking around Marzipan Man's feet, making him rock even more. It was difficult for him to aim and he began to fire at random. Great gobbets of marzipan splatted against the walls, floor and ceiling, sometimes splattering his own troops.

The Christmas Fairy was beside herself, jerking and twisting more and more crazily. 'Where's my Dove of Peace!' she screamed. 'Splatter them! Splat them to bits!'

The bird swooped across the room and dropped a splatter bomb. It hit the tube behind the troops but failed to do anything other than knock everyone off their feet for a moment. They were soon back at work and the Dove came in on another bombing run.

Max was now at the cupboard door, watching the battle that still raged. It was a touch-and-go situation. If Ellie and the tube gang got a direct hit that would be it. The plan would fail. But how could he take out the Dove of Peace?

Max raced round the edge of the room, occasionally fighting his way past a rebel warrior, until he reached their old HQ. Once inside he hurried straight across to a camouflaged toy helicopter. Switching on the power, the 'copter lit up all over as its rotor blades whizzed into action.

Max lifted from the ground, turned the chopper towards the sliding door and neatly clattered out into the thick of the battle. He zoomed into the air, scattering angels in every direction. He wheeled round to seek out the Dove and soon the two of them were locked in

a dogfight, with Max spraying the Dove with
hundreds and thousands, trying to stop it from
dropping any further bombs.

Meanwhile Ellie was still urging her elephant
forward, dragging the vacuum cleaner nozzle and
sucking away at Marzipan Man. The power of
the vacuum was so strong that flecks of marzipan
began to be stripped away from the giant's feet
and vanish up the tube. The flecks soon became
blobs, which became great lumps of the revolting
stuff. Marzipan Man began to slowly collapse as

more and more marzipan disappeared from his lower body and got sucked inside the vacuum cleaner. It really had become a monster.

'No!' screeched the Christmas Fairy. 'My magnificent Marzipan Man, all going up the spout! It's not fair! Stop! Stop! My troops! Where are you? Fight them! Destroy them!'

But at that moment Marzipan Man began his last, slow collapse. Like a tower block being demolished, he disintegrated from the bottom up, spilling hundreds of snowmen to the ground where they landed, splat, in the spreading slop of marzipan.

In the final stage of collapse an enormous wave of marzipan was sent racing across the floor like a tsunami. It caught up the Christmas Fairy on its crest and was only stopped when it reached the wall.

SPLOPP!!

The Christmas Fairy found herself stuck firmly halfway up the wall. To add insult to injury she was immediately bombed by her own Dove of Peace. Max had finally fired off the chopper's twin liquorice torpedoes and scored a direct hit. The Dove went into a spiral dive, crashing into the wall just above the Christmas Fairy and releasing its entire payload of splatter bombs on top of her head.

The battle was over. The battle was won.

14 More Marzipan.
Is This the End?

When Father Christmas walked into the
Christmas Shop he was shocked to say the least.

'This place has been hit by a tornado,' he
muttered crossly, picking his way gingerly across
the floor in search of toys for his sack.

Ellie and Max peeped out from behind the sliding door. There he was, Father Christmas himself!

'What do we do now?' asked Max. 'It's Christmas and we're not home. We're stuck here for ever, aren't we?'

But Ellie was studying her pyjamas. Surely they would come to the rescue? After all, it was the Cosmic Pyjamas that had brought them both here. It was the Cosmic Pyjamas that had provided them with that stick of dynamite just at the right moment. And it was the Cosmic Pyjamas that had twice sent them important messages. Surely they would take them home?

That was when the little picture of their house appeared. Ellie grabbed Max and showed him. He wasn't impressed.

'It's only a picture,' he complained. 'It's not doing anything and we're still here.'

Ellie had more faith. She knew it was time to say goodbye to Blondie, Aysha and all their new friends. That was hard, because they had fought a massive battle together, they had survived and, above all, they had won.

'Can't thank you enough,' said Blondie. 'I 'ave to say I thought you were a bit of a – what do you call it in your world? A prawn?'

'Prat?' suggested Ellie, with a little giggle.

'Yeah. That's what I thought when you arrived. But you've both been brilliant.'

Aysha peered out at Father Christmas and grinned. 'We're free to leave at last,' she said. 'Any minute now Father Christmas will come in here and pick us up for his sack. We shall be free and everyone can have Christmas. And that's thanks to you and Max.'

'Max!' cried Ellie. 'Look at the windows on the house!' Ellie lifted her sleeve. The picture was still there, quivering, but now, at the windows, Mum and Dad were waving to them.

'We have to go,' said Ellie hastily. 'It's our moment.' She held Max's hand tightly and

PHWOOOOOSH!!!!!

They were whirling and swirling, spinning
round and round until FWUMMPPP!

They landed with a bang on the landing
between their bedrooms. They hardly had time
to recover before Dad poked a tousled, grumpy
head out of his bedroom.

'Do you have to make so much noise? I know
it's Christmas morning but it's only five o' clock!
If you wake your mother up she'll turn you into
mince pies! Now, get back to bed, you scamps.'
Dad pulled his head back in and shut the door.

Ellie and Max looked at each other for a moment and then burst out laughing. They disappeared into their rooms and discovered that Father Christmas had left two rather fat stockings. They were both exhausted, but not so tired that they couldn't open half the stocking contents before they fell asleep.

Mum and Dad had to wake them up for breakfast, and then it was Christmas proper, with the handing out of presents. Among Ellie's gifts was a Lara Croft doll.

'Where's her handbag?' Max asked.

Mum shook her head and laughed. 'Lara Croft doesn't have a handbag!'

Ellie didn't say anything, but she was already planning to dye the doll's hair blonde.

Max was cuddling a large grey dinosaur. 'This is Dippy,' he announced.

'Right,' smiled Dad. 'Have you found the button under his tummy yet?'

'What button – whoa! Hey, that is so cool!'
Max had pressed the button and the diplodocus
had given his tail an enormous flick. 'Wow! You
could knock plugs into sockets with a tail like
that!'

Mum and Dad exchanged looks. First it was
handbags for Lara Croft and now Max wanted
to knock plugs into sockets with a dinosaur's tail.
What planet was Max on?

Later, after Christmas lunch, Max and Ellie
had a long talk with each other about whether

or not they should tell their parents what had happened to them.

'They won't believe us whatever we say,' Ellie pointed out.

'I expect they'll tell us it was a dream,' Max grumbled. 'But it wasn't because my legs still hurt a bit from those stings.'

'Me too,' nodded Ellie. 'We'll just keep quiet then.'

As evening approached, Mum brought out her special Christmas cake. She plonked it down on the table and the children eyed it suspiciously. There was a faint smell hanging over the cake, a smell that was familiar to them both.

Marzipan.

Max and Ellie said they didn't want any Christmas cake. Christmas was much better without marzipan, they said, so Mum gave them a mince pie each. Max took the top off his and examined the inside by pushing the thin end of his spoon into the contents and rummaging around.

'Do you have to play with your food like that?'
demanded Dad. 'What on earth are you doing?'

'Just checking,' muttered Max. He felt Ellie's
foot pressing against his leg under the table and
he smiled. Ellie understood.

After tea the children went and looked at
the Christmas tree. The angels hanging on the
branch ends looked quite – well, angelic really.

And the fairy on top of the Christmas tree had two eyes and seemed quite happy to be there. Ellie gave a relieved sigh and told Max that Lara Blondie was smiling.

'Yeah, maybe,' he grunted.

'What's the matter with you?' Ellie asked.

'I was just thinking, that's all. I was thinking, dinosaurs are OK – I mean I do *like* Dippy, he's great – but I was thinking a helicopter, one that I could fly – that would really be something!'

Several months later Mum found the Cosmic Pyjamas lying at the very bottom of one of Ellie's drawers. Mum folded them neatly and took them to the charity shop.

'You only ever wore them once,' she told Ellie later that day.

'I know,' Ellie agreed. 'I never knew what they were going to do.'

Mum gave a chuckle and tousled Ellie's hair. 'You're such a strange creature sometimes. You say the oddest things. Pyjamas aren't supposed to do anything, they're just – well, pyjamas.'

'Whatever,' shrugged Ellie. 'Anyhow, they've gone now.' She felt quite relieved.

However, although the pyjamas had disappeared from Max and Ellie's life it was definitely not the last that would be heard of the Cosmic Pyjamas.

If you see them, no matter where – BEWARE! These pyjamas could damage your Life!

Ask Jeremy

Of all the books you have written, which one is your favourite?

I loved writing both **KRAZY KOW SAVES THE WORLD – WELL, ALMOST** and **STUFF**, my first book for teenagers. Both these made me laugh out loud while I was writing and I was pleased with the overall result in each case. I also love writing the stories about Nicholas and his daft family – **MY DAD**, **MY MUM**, **MY BROTHER** and so on.

If you couldn't be a writer what would you be?

Well, I'd be pretty fed up for a start, because writing was the one thing I knew I wanted to do from the age of nine onward. But if I DID have to do something else, I would love to be either an accomplished pianist or an artist of some sort. Music and art have played a big part in my whole life and I would love to be involved in them in some way.

What's the best thing about writing stories?

Oh dear – so many things to say here! Getting paid for making things up is pretty high on the list! It's also something you do on your own, inside your own head – nobody can interfere with that. The only boss you have is yourself. And you are creating something that nobody else has made before you. I also love making my readers laugh and want to read more and more.

Did you ever have a nightmare teacher?
(And who was your best ever?)

My nightmare at primary school was Mrs Chappell, long since dead. I knew her secret – she was not actually human. She was a Tyrannosaurus rex in disguise. She taught me for two years when I was in Y5 and Y6, and we didn't like each other at all. My best ever was when I was in Y3 and Y4. Her name was Miss Cox, and she was the one who first encouraged me to write stories. She was brilliant. Sadly, she is long dead too.

When you were a kid you used to play kiss-chase. Did you always do the chasing or did anyone ever chase you?!

I usually did the chasing, but when I got chased, I didn't bother to run very fast! Maybe I shouldn't admit to that! We didn't play kiss-chase at school – it was usually played during holidays. If we had tried playing it at school we would have been in serious trouble. Mind you, I seemed to spend most of my time in trouble of one sort or another, so maybe it wouldn't have mattered that much.

Puffin by Post

Battle for Christmas – Jeremy Strong

If you have enjoyed this book and want to read more,
then check out these other great Puffin titles.
You can order any of the following books direct with Puffin by Post:

Krazy Kow Saves the World – Well, Almost • 9780141322391	£4.99
'Superb . . . no udder book will do' – *Observer*	

The Hundred-Mile-an-Hour Dog • Jeremy Strong • 9780141322346	£4.99
Winner of the Children's Book Award	

Beware! Killer Tomatoes • Jeremy Strong • 9780141320588	£4.99
'His books crackle with good humour and invention' – *TES*	

My Brother's Famous Bottom • Jeremy Strong • 9780141319780	£4.99
'A real talent for silliness and slapstick' – *The Sunday Times*	

Let's Do the Pharaoh • Jeremy Strong • 9780141316802	£4.99
'Comedy and general fizz are Jeremy Strong's trademark' – *Independent*	

Just contact:

Puffin Books, C/o Bookpost, PO Box 29,
Douglas, Isle of Man, IM99 1BQ
Credit cards accepted. For further details:
Telephone: 01624 677237
Fax: 01624 670923

You can email your orders to: bookshop@enterprise.net
Or order online at: www.bookpost.co.uk

Free delivery in the UK.
Overseas customers must add £2 per book.

Prices and availability are subject to change.

Visit puffin.co.uk to find out about the latest titles, read extracts and
exclusive author interviews, and enter exciting competitions.
You can also browse thousands of Puffin books online.